ZACHARY'S NEW HOME

A Story for Foster and Adopted Children

**by Geraldine M. Blomquist, M.S.W.
& Paul B. Blomquist**

illustrated by Margo Lemieux

MAGINATION PRESS · NEW YORK

To our families, to Ken Crosby, and
to the foster parents and children
of Adams County, and in memory of
Mary Molettiere and Arnold Blomquist

Library of Congress Cataloging-in-Publication Data
Blomquist, Geraldine Molettiere.
    Zachary's new home : a story for foster and adopted children / by
Geraldine Molettiere Blomquist and Paul B. Blomquist ; illustrated
by Margo Lemieux.
    p.   cm.
    Summary: Zachary still remembers his "real" parents and finds that
adjusting to life as Marie and Tom's adopted son is sometimes a
painful reality.
    ISBN 0-945354-28-2. — ISBN 0-945354-27-4 (pbk.)
    [1. Adoption—Fiction.   2. Foster home care—Fiction.]
I. Blomquist, Paul B.   II. Lemieux, Margo, ill.   III. Title.
PZ7.B6222Zac   1990
[E]—dc20   90-41914
                                                   CIP
                                                   AC

Distributed in Canada by Book Center, 1140 Beaulac St., Montreal, Quebec H4R 1R8, Canada

Newbridge Book Clubs. For information about our audio products, write us at:
Newbridge Book Clubs, 3000 Cindel Drive, Delran, NJ 08370.

Manufactured in the United States of America

10 9 8 7 6 5 4 3 2 1

Introduction for Foster and Adoptive Parents

Children in foster care, whether they remain with foster parents or are eventually adopted, have usually suffered many painful separations. They are taken from dysfunctional or disrupted families and placed with strangers for reasons they may not understand. They may be sent to as many as four different homes before a permanent arrangement is made, and may exhibit serious behavioral problems. They are generally very confused, angry, and sad.

Foster and adoptive parents often experience a great deal of stress and confusion themselves in trying to manage these children. They usually find it helpful to be prepared with an understanding of what behaviors to expect.

Zachary's New Home explores the experiences, problems, and emotions of the young foster or adopted child. It is designed to be read to children aged 3 to 8 by foster parents, adoptive parents, social workers, therapists, or counselors. The comforting text and illustrations help children cope with the many losses and changes in their lives. Since the main character in the story exhibits the type of disruptive behavior that often prevents placement from proceeding smoothly, the story provides insight to foster and adoptive parents as well.

This story may evoke strong emotions in foster or adopted children. It is important that knowledgeable and concerned adults discuss these with the children, allowing them to explore their own feelings. After reading the book, it would also be helpful for the parents or counselors to provide nurturing activities, reassurance, and love, thus sustaining and encouraging the children's optimism about their future.

Zachary and his mother had fun together.
Sometimes Zachary's mother read to him.
Sometimes she played games with him.

Zachary and his dad had fun together, too.
Sometimes they went for walks in the mountains.
His dad also played games with Zachary.

Then something happened, and Zachary didn't
see his dad anymore. His mom didn't play with him
or read to him anymore, either. She was mad a lot
of the time. Sometimes she was so mad she hit
Zachary.

One day, Zachary's mom had a visitor named Sarah. Sarah talked to Zachary's mom. She also talked to Zachary. She told him he could not live with his mother anymore. Sarah was going to take him to another home to live.

On the way to the foster home, Sarah told Zachary that children need safe homes where they will not be hurt, where they are not left alone, where they receive loving care and attention. Even though his mother loved him, she had many problems. She tried to take care of Zachary, but she could not give him the kind of care he needed.

Zachary remembered the times his mother hurt him.

The foster home frightened Zachary. He didn't know anyone there, and the children were all very different from him. They had one thing in common, though—they were not living with their parents.

Sarah told Zachary he would stay here until she could find him a new home, with a new mom and a new dad.

"I don't want a new mom and a new dad," thought Zachary, "I want the mom and dad I had."

In bed that night, Zachary cried quietly to himself.
He was very sad. He wished he could stay with his
mom. He thought about what he did wrong to take
him away from her, but he did not understand.
He was very lonely.

Some nights Zachary had bad dreams. He dreamed that he was all alone in the woods looking for something. He never finished the dream, but woke up feeling scared.

A few months later, Sarah took Zachary to court. A judge looked down from his bench. He said, "We have a new family for you, Zachary."

Zachary was kind of happy and kind of scared. Most of all, though, he wished he could see his "real" mom and dad.

Sarah took Zachary into a small room next to the courtroom. She said, "Zachary, these are your new parents, Tom and Marie. You will live with them now. They want to take care of you."

Zachary looked at them and tried to smile, but deep down he felt sure he did not want to go with them.

Tom and Marie said, "We hope you will be happy with us. We know our house will be new to you, but we will try to help you feel at home. You can call us Mom and Dad if you want to."

Zachary did not want to.

The first couple of days were a little hard because Zachary did not know the rules of the house. But once he got used to it, he started to have fun.

Tom and Marie were nice. Marie played games with him. Sometimes she read to him. Tom took Zachary to the mountains. Sometimes all three of them played games together.

Zachary was getting along well with Tom and Marie. But sometimes he felt angry. He did not know why. He could not concentrate in school. Every day Zachary got in trouble. He couldn't seem to help it.

One day in school, Zachary got into a fight with another boy in the lunch line. His teacher called Marie. When Zachary got home, Marie sent him to his room.

That night, Zachary heard Tom and Marie talking. Marie said, "I didn't know Zachary would be so difficult. He keeps getting into trouble."

Tom said, "It must be very hard for Zachary to lose his mom and dad. It could be he is mad about losing them."

"He does seem upset," agreed Marie, "but sometimes he makes me so angry. It seems our loving him is not enough."

Zachary was very unhappy. Tom and Marie were mad at him. He thought about his "real" mom and dad. He wished he were still with them. Then he had an idea. Maybe he could find his parents.

The next day, instead of going to school, Zachary went looking for his mom and dad.

After searching for his mother's house all day, Zachary was tired and hungry. And, he was lost. It was as if his bad dream had come true.

He sat down and cried. "Mom and Dad don't want me, and neither do Tom and Marie. Nobody does."

A policeman heard Zachary crying. He asked
Zachary if he needed help. Zachary told him what
had happened. The policeman took Zachary home
to Tom and Marie.

Tom and Marie were very happy to see him. "Zachary," they cried, "we were so worried. We searched all over town for you. We are so glad you are home."

Zachary was very hungry. Marie made him his
favorite kind of sandwich.

Then Zachary took a warm bath. When he finished,
Tom rubbed him dry with a big fluffy towel.

Zachary was glad to be back safe with Tom and Marie.

"Zachary," said Tom, "we love you very much. We know you are not happy right now, and we want to help you feel better."

"We know you miss your parents," Marie added. "It's OK for you to think about them. And maybe someday you can visit them. But we are very happy you are here with us now."

Zachary was so tired he fell asleep on Tom's lap.
Tom stayed very still. Zachary slept for a long time.
He smiled as he dreamed. Zachary dreamed he had
found a new home.